JACOB'S BALLOON

Matthew W. Bertsch

Bloodborne Publishing

Published by
Bloodborne Publishing
P.O. Box 50101
Denton, TX 76206

ISBN: 978-0-6151-5164-9

Printed in the United States of America

April 2007

For those who hurt and *feel* alone

Jacob's Balloon

1

IT ALWAYS AMAZED Jacob that the combination of the same few ingredients could produce such a wide variety of beers. After all, how many different mixtures and processes can there be in fermenting hops, barley, malt and whatnot? Yet each recipe can be distinctly called beer. It kind of went along the lines of the "seed" thought he had earlier; perhaps not quite as deep, but nonetheless a mystery on the surface. Ah yes, seeds, amazing little things.

How is it that a seed eventually turns into an apple or a grape? A tiny seed, bedded in and feeding from the dirt becomes a tree or a vine which produces the fruit. An apple and a grape come from the same soil, the same rain and the same sunlight, but the end results are completely unique. The only difference is the starting point: the seed. And another thing...from where in the dirt does the fruit get its sweetness?

Worms eat that same dirt, he thought, *but I'll have the fruit salad, thank you!*

Such thoughts weren't going to solve the issue of poverty nor cure cancer or bring world peace...but then again, they weren't meant to. They were simply something to occupy Jacob's mind each night as he closed up Pete's Liquor Store. Without such thoughts, a man could go insane from the mindless routine: mop the floors, stock the shelves, make sure the receiving door in the back is padlocked, stock the coolers, count the drawer, and drop the cash. The random, pointless thoughts were welcomed. He enjoyed such daily diversions. They carried him away from reality, if only for a few moments. Everyone needed that sort of downtime. Jacob's days were filled with classes at Purdue; *they* dictated his topics. But nighttime was *his* time.

It was almost peaceful now, back behind the glass restocking the chilled beverages. The temperature was nice and cool, the sort of climate that only a Yankee could appreciate. Tonight was much like the others: going through the checklist of duties, unwinding, assisting the occasional last-minute party-hound; thinking. It was just like all those other nights...at least up to this point.

It was hard to say just how long the guy had been waiting at the register when Jacob finally noticed him. Sometimes when Jacob let his mind wander like this, his customer service skills suffered. One time there was an entire sorority wandering through the store for five minutes before he even realized they were there.

Peering between the bottles from inside the cooler, Jacob almost missed a very important clue concerning his latest customer. He *almost* missed it. It wasn't the trench coat the man wore; such attire in an Indiana college town, even in the early nineties, wasn't too uncommon. It wasn't that this man was way too old and far too worn to be hanging out near a college campus; he was definitely *not* a student. No, it wasn't even that. Instead, it was the metallic cylinder sticking out the bottom of his trench coat that nearly missed Jacob's eye. It appeared to be, he surmised, a 12-gauge, sawed-off shotgun. Unfortunately for the scumbag holding it, not 'sawed-off' enough.

Jacob had never been through a robbery before, but it was bound to happen sooner or later in this line of business.

What to do?

Out front, the scruffy-looking man who had been looking around nervously for the past few moments finally stopped rapping his knuckles on the counter and abruptly slammed down his fist. He reached across to the till, upending several small novelty displays in the process, and began pounding at the register's buttons. Several attempts were hastily made between frantic glances; none produced the greens. Perhaps the man should have taken a different career path somewhere along the line. At the very least he should have included a brief tour as a "transaction accountant" at a fast-food restaurant. The skills acquired from a position like that could have proven real handy just about now (not to mention the fact that having a job might have made this whole ordeal unnecessary to begin with). The man's probing was far from surgical and became increasingly violent. His hammering on the drawer increased in tempo and intensity. Suddenly he heard a crash behind him.

It was Jacob, with a bag of peanuts clenched in his teeth, a lime wedged under his chin and a couple of cases of beer in tow; one of which had just slipped from his hand. Stiffly, he bent down to retrieve it. His actions were slow, deliberate and determined. He used his foot and knee to hike the fallen case back into his hand for a firm handle. He looked much like a robot in his maneuvers, under the heavy weight of all he carried. Jacob continued down the aisle, shuffling along as if looking for further items of interest. The man at the counter was wide-eyed and frozen in mid-strike. When he finally "noticed" the man, Jacob dropped his jaw and, consequently, the lime and the peanuts.

"Oh sh...uh, do you work here, man?" Jacob said.

The two stood staring nervously at each other for a moment. Jacob's mind was racing nearly as fast as his heart. He was in the poker match of his life...and possibly *for* his life. The two men studied each other, looking for tell signs. Who was bluffing? Perhaps neither. Jacob probed the stranger's soul with his senses, looking for any sign of wariness or disbelief. He saw nothing, just confusion. The man finally shrugged his shoulders and shook his head.

Jacob sensed that he had the thief at his mercy, so he went all in.

"Dude, I think the store's abandoned...I'm gonna grab and go! Shit, man, help yourself!"

With this, Jacob gathered the items he had dropped, added a couple packs of jerky and bolted for the front door. The dazed thief, after playing connect-the-dots for a moment, started to celebrate. He limped to a more comfortable position behind the counter to get a better look at the stupid machine.

In this less affluent part of town, on the outskirts of the University, all of the buildings had bars on the doors and windows. Pete's was no exception. Rich, the proprietor, was as frugal as any other small business owner, but he also understood the importance of protecting his investment. Thankfully for tonight, he was also reasonable.

A few short weeks earlier, Jacob had asked Rich to remove the manual locks from the inside of the store doors.

"The only person who needs to be able to lock the doors," Jacob had explained to his boss, "is the person who holds the keys.

After all, what's the first thing that happens in the movies when a criminal comes into a convenience store? We've all seen it a hundred times before: they lock the front door behind them and turn the sign to "Closed". It's one less "front" to worry about while pulling off the job."

When Jacob made this suggestion he had really had no idea just how useful the modification was going to be.

Trench Coat Man was just about to make some real progress on getting the goods when he was faced with another surprise: the tumbling grind of a commercial door being locked. As the would be thief stared at the doors – not so welcoming now as they had seemed just ten minutes ago – he realized what had happened. He had been played. Now he was a sitting duck. His heart seemed to stop in his chest and beads of sweat instantly sprouted from his forehead. It dawned on him that the police would most likely be arriving shortly.

"Damn!"

Outside, Jacob bent down, put his hands on his knees and took a few, much needed and previously suppressed deep breaths. After a quick rest, he grabbed one of the cold cases he had set aside while locking the door and began to head for a nearby payphone. Two steps into his journey Jacob heard a series of loud and paralyzing "booms". Showers of sparks and jagged glass peppered his previous position. The captive was shooting out the doors and windows. The bars, however, would ultimately prove impassable for him. The rear entry had been padlocked earlier in the night; no more deliveries were expected. The wannabe criminal was, in effect, already in custody.

Jacob was digging in his pocket for coins when he remembered that they weren't needed for an emergency call. His adrenaline-pumped fingers shook as he pressed 911.

After making the call, Jacob sat atop the case of beer and tried to lower his pulse. He heard the man inside the cage screaming and cursing and essentially trashing the place; trying to figure out how to free himself. Jacob floated an instinctual prayer, *God don't let him get to me.* Since the captive had spent his few shells trying to blast his way out of the store, Jacob figured the authorities wouldn't have much of a struggle on their hands when they finally arrived.

The craftiness of Man, Jacob thought as he sat waiting, *is a two-way street.* It's unfortunate that selfishness, deviancy...and yes, even poverty and need existed to begin with. But as long as they *do* exist, so must balance. It was idealistic of Jacob to think things could be any different, but things *should* be different.

Why can't the world be the one I knew as a child?

2

THERE HAD never been a more beautiful day in all of young Jacob's life. A light mist still covering the grass sparkled like a kaleidoscope from the sun's rays. The dew droplets looked like purple, green, pink and yellow glitter sprinkled on the lawn. The air was crisp and, in the distance, you could still see a hazy fog hovering over the ground. The orange eastern sky faded to blue overhead and the few clouds looked like patches of flour, scattered.

Jacob loved Leo Elementary. There was so much to do, so much new, and he had lots of friends. It was great! He especially liked recess and playing kickball in gym class.

"Slow and bouncy, slooooow and bouncy". That's how Jacob told Mr. Karr to pitch the kickball when he was up. It was the best pitch to kick a long way. Maybe, if he was lucky, it would even be a home run.

Leo was a small town, and quiet; not at all like the city. Sometimes Jacob liked going to the mall in Fort Wayne, but it was better in the country. It was a good place to live. The Amish thought so, too. They lived out here and *never* went into town. They were a little different, the Amish, but they were good people. They spoke English too, even though it sounded a little funny. Sometimes Jacob's Amish classmates would say words that sounded so strange that he couldn't understand them. They would be saying normal words and then all of a sudden throw in some gibberish. After time, though, Jacob began to understand some of their words and phrases. If one of them would tell his younger brother to "be-schtill", that meant for him to shut-up!

The folks in the country were nice. They cared about each other and waved to everyone. People would stop to chat with each other – even with the visitors. You could always tell who wasn't from around here because they asked a lot of questions. They looked like they were at the zoo or something; especially when they saw the Amish. They pointed a lot and smiled and sometimes they even laughed.

The Pledge of Allegiance and Morning Prayer had already been recited. Principal Runzlig had just finished the daily announcements over the intercom, bringing all the little "Leo Lions" up to speed. All that stuff took forever. There were more important things to do today! It was like a Christmas morning; the presents begging to be let out. But no, gotta eat some breakfast first. Eggs take *so long* to cook on Christmas morning. That's what today was like. Waiting! Except now it wasn't waiting for Mom and Dad to get ready to open presents, it was getting through all the routine stuff that Teacher and Principal had to do every morning. Couldn't they just skip all that today?

It was going to be the best day ever. No reading or writing today. Today, English class was going to be special. And it was almost time: Teacher almost had the balloons ready to go!

8

Mrs. Courier was the best fourth-grade teacher ever. Every fall, she gave each of her students a small piece of paper that she had prepared and had him or her cover it in plastic wrap and stick it inside a helium balloon. On each piece of paper was the child's name and parent's home address. She did this so her class could find pen pals to write to. To Mrs. Courier, it was an exciting way to help her class improve their writing skills; to Jacob...well, he just liked balloons. The note thing was pretty cool too. It would be like his very own message in a bottle. Where would it go? Who would find it?

Just the day before, Mrs. Courier told the class stories from previous years when students sent out their balloons. Last year a bunch of the kids got letters back from all over the place. One time, a girl named Lisa even got a letter from Pennsylvania. That was two states away! When Teacher told those stories it was hard to pay attention. Jacob dreamed about how his balloon was going to go farther than anyone else's...ever! *His* balloon would fly *higher* than ever; go *faster* than all the others. Maybe *his* balloon would even go all the way to Canada!

Jacob never had a pen pal before. He couldn't wait to tell that person all about himself. He could talk about how he likes puppies. He could write that he likes stories about Jesus. He could say that his favorite color is orange; but his pen pal would probably already know that, because he picked an orange balloon.

Now the classroom was a madhouse. The children were wrapping up their cards, sealing them watertight and stuffing them into their balloons. At the front of the class, Mrs. Courier was double-checking everything, then filling the balloons with floaty gas and tying them off with a string. Each string had a loop on the end to go around the owner's wrist so no one would accidentally launch his or her balloon too soon.

Jacob finished stuffing his balloon. He did it perfectly. The plastic wrap was nice and smooth, sealed down nice and tight. There really wasn't a whole lot he could have messed up – it already had his name and address preprinted on the paper that Mrs. Courier prepared earlier from the school records. Even so, no one could have done a better job than Jacob did.

He hurried to the front of the class to have his balloon filled and tied to his wrist. Jacob watched Mrs. Courier as she checked everything. She was pretty and always had a smile on her face. She must have been real proud of Jacob for doing everything right. Teacher was real careful when she filled his balloon, making sure she didn't pop it. He looked at her shiny red nails as she slipped the loop over his hand. She finished it for him flawlessly; his balloon was the best in the class. Jacob loved her!

The stories she told the day before made it tough for any of the children to sleep the previous night. Jacob was so excited, though, that he didn't even notice how tired he really was. The time was here at last. Everyone was ready and lined up, single file, at the door. Jacob fought to get as close to the front of the line as he could. The sooner he got outdoors, he thought, the sooner he could release his balloon.

The stairway and halls leading outside to the playground were much longer than Jacob remembered. Sometime between this morning and now, someone must have sneaked in and stretched the entire pathway leading to the outside. Luckily, the row of rainbow-colored balloons following him looked like a Chinese dragon parade, and the thought distracted him just enough to make it through the long journey.

Finally all forty-three fourth graders were out on the school lawn. A couple of the boys let their balloons fly before Teacher said it was ok. Jacob nearly did the same, but he bit his lip and wiggled his one knee back and forth; that seemed to help. Mrs. Courier wouldn't have been real happy with him if he let his balloon go too early, and he didn't want to upset her.

At last, Teacher gave the ok.

Orange was Jacob's favorite color and his balloon was the perfect shade of orange. He watched it intensely, trying to follow it as it weaved its way through the crowd of rising balloons. Smaller and smaller they became and all too soon the tiny dots were out of sight.

3

PURDUE UNIVERSITY was established in 1869 atop the bluffs of the winding Wabash River in the west-central Indiana town of West Lafayette. The school's founder, John Purdue, is buried to this day at the foot of the steps leading up to the original University building. There have been stories how his grave has been robbed on numerous occasions – stories that on one Halloween night his body was exhumed and placed, sitting upright, on one of the buildings' steps. But those are, most likely, just legends and his body truly rests in peace.

The school is most often noted for turning out scientists of all sorts: agriculturalists, astronauts, engineers, veterinarians, and the like. Of course, not every student majors in a science there. Being a state-funded institution, Purdue offers the full spectrum of study as well.

The University has its share of notable names associated with it, including Alumni Neil Armstrong and Gene Cernan, the first and last men to walk on the moon. Former President Benjamin Harrison served on its board of advisors many years ago. Among the list of famous graduates there's also Orville Redenbacher who pops to mind. Even Kermit the Frog received his proper name from one of the school's beloved professors.

Amelia Earhart was a faculty member there for a season, until to her fateful adventure. There is little doubt that the rival Indiana Hoosiers formulated a handful of jabs surrounding her connection with the institution and "getting lost." But with just as much certainty, such "courtesies" had been returned, in fair balance, over the years.

Jacob didn't consciously pick Purdue based on its impressive list of accolades. Rather, he ended up there by default. In retrospect, he was glad he did.

He began his study at one of the school's satellite extensions in Fort Wayne. IPFW was a hybrid of both Purdue and Indiana Universities. Its staff and administration was associated with both Universities. Once Jacob finally figured out what he wanted to major in, that choice ultimately determined which school he belonged to.

Coming from a modest (but certainly adequate and loving) home, Jacob shouldered much of the cost of his education. Thankfully, he was able to live with his mother while starting out to avoid the cost of housing. While at the extension, he worked as a Bell Captain at one of the city's corporate hotels; earning enough to help cover his tuition, books and even some extra "fun money" along the way. But he always knew the day would eventually come when he would have to "board the mother ship" to complete his study.

After a few years, Jacob had completed most of his required courses and managed to save up enough to finish his electives at the main campus. He still needed to earn some day-to-day money by working at a nearby liquor store, but he now had things mapped out to pay for everything and get his degree within the year. Now he was on the main campus; in the big leagues. Soon he would have his bachelor's degree in Communications: the trophy that he had worked for so hard.

It was fall; Jacob's favorite time of the year. Sugar maple leaves, dried by the cool autumn air, were the most beautiful of all of fall's decorations. He often sat beneath Purdue's glorious trees as he wrote letters back home to his mother. He preferred writing to his mother over calling her on the phone. There was a certain power to the written word that Jacob liked.

A phone conversation is soon forgotten, but a letter is so...permanent; so eternal, he thought.

In his letters, Jacob always told his mother how special she was to him; how he loved her. He assured his mother that all was well; the job was going well, he was going to classes and getting good grades. His mother would reply often by phone or in writing, telling him how proud she was of her son. She was forever optimistic. When Jacob wrote her, he tried to avoid interjecting any of the negativity or frustrations he often felt. Though he made the conscious effort to avoid worrying his mother, somehow *something* alarming always seemed to find its way into his message. He just couldn't seem to control that. How could he pour out his heart onto the paper – how could he be honest and transparent with his mother – without including at least *some* of the turmoil that was inside? She knew her boy, so he guessed it was OK to let a little of that pain come out. One thing was certain, though: in his latest letter he wasn't going to tell her that he was nearly robbed just the other night.

No, Jake didn't want to worry his mother, so he never revealed to her everything he was going through; he didn't express *everything* he felt. The fact was that as he grew older and gained more life experiences, he began to realize that the world was not the utopia he knew as a boy...but he didn't need to add that burden onto his mother's shoulders.

Over the years, Jacob's heart became quite hardened. The world, he found, was full of selfish and unforgiving people. Jacob decided that every problem on this earth was a result of two main vices: selfishness and lack of forgiveness. Whether it be racism, greed, vindictiveness...every vile thing on this earth has its roots in these two evils.

Still, something inside of Jacob drove him to seek out hope. He knew there were still some good people; people like his mother and father. *You have to keep that balance.*

It was Wednesday afternoon. Jacob sat, trying to clear his mind; trying to find peace. He stared out across the courtyard, watching the other students. Some were studying in the grass. Others were just soaking up the last rays of the waning season's sun. The lawn was full of all sorts of people. Some were alone. Others were grouped together with their buddies. He even saw Pastor Jack in one corner of the lawn, preaching his standard "fire and brimstone" message. Jacob often wondered if Pastor really thought he was being effective. What he was saying could have all been true, technically. Still, there's something to be said for tact, compassion and understanding. While Jacob couldn't hear the missionary's exact words from where he was sitting, he really didn't need to. He had heard the man's message several times before. There was no mystery to what the "man of God" was speaking.

"If ya don't turn from ya evil way-uhs...you'll baaaaarn with the demons-uh!"

Jacob grew up in the church and even though he sometimes questioned his beliefs, he always maintained his relationship with God and cherished it deep in his core. He wondered if people like Jack ever ventured into the real world to see what *really* went on. "Be in the world, but not *of* the world." It seems like some folks only read half of that statement: "Be not *of* the world." They seem to forget to also be *in* it. Sure, Pastor Jack was *standing* "in the world", but he wasn't really *in* it. His eyes and ears were perfectly healthy, but he was blind and deaf. Only his mouth seemed to be both functional and active.

If you're going to preach to these *people,* Jacob thought, *preach some encouragement. Preach some hope! Preach some love! The diamond can be polished later, but at this point it's still buried in the dirt!*

Dirt...how fascinating it is if you really, *really* think about it. How incredible it is and yet how forgettable and bland it is at the same time. It's so wonderful. It's so horrid.

Jacob was reminded of the Donkey Story his pastor had preached a few years back: Once, when a donkey was walking through a pasture, he fell into a deep hole. No matter what he did or how hard he tried, the poor donkey just couldn't get himself up and out of the hole. He was in too deep. After awhile – just when the donkey thought things couldn't get any worse – he felt something fall onto his back. It was dirt. Some of the farmhands were filling in the hole so no one would fall into it and get injured. The donkey couldn't believe it. At first he thought he was going to simply die alone of starvation inside this hole – a bad enough way to go. Now, though, it appeared he was going to be buried alive. Wonderful! The donkey tried his best to make some noise, hoping someone would hear him and help him out of the hole. No one came to his rescue. No one listened to him. No one even heard him. Down came another shovelful, landing again on the donkey's back. Not knowing what else to do, the donkey shook the dirt off his back and stepped on it. Another load of dirt, another shake-off, another dirt-stamping. He just kept shaking it off and stamping on it because he didn't know what else to do. Pretty soon, the donkey realized something: as each measure of dirt came down and he got on top of it, he continued to rise. It wasn't long before the donkey discovered he was no longer in a hole.

There you go Mr. Preacher man, Jacob thought, *start off with something like that! And when you preach it, understand that it's not always easy to just shake off the dirt either.*

"Ya know, Jack, I could really use your help," Jacob said to himself, "A lot of us could use your help. But you're only helping yourself...and you're really not doing that very well either."

Jacob often thought about the Donkey Story. It's not easy to let go of the past. It's not easy to just shake it off. But he always tried to look forward; to look for hope. He tried.

Without a doubt, the past was difficult for Jacob to manage. It was difficult to lose his father, especially at the age when he needed him most. The past held so many painful things: failures, mistakes, and...lost love.

4

NIGHTFALL WAS NOW sitting with Jacob; not as much sitting with him as encompassing him. It gave him no comfort. It held him without concern. His on-campus apartment's bedroom was pitch black. It was the sort of blackness that a blind man would see with eyes wide open, even on a sunny day. The silence of his room was only interrupted by the thumping bass of a few cranked stereos and some occasional "woops" made elsewhere, outside his four walls. The noises were muffled and sounded to Jacob as if he was underwater, hearing them above the surface. They weren't distracting, though; they were easily ignored. His thoughts, on the other hand, were loud in his head. *They* were like the drops from a leaky faucet that simply would not cease. Sleep – peace – would not come easy tonight.

It happened on a cold, wet January night about two years earlier. He had arrived at Marie's house moments ago and was now standing in her bedroom. Marie, sitting on her bed, had tears streaming down her cheeks. Jacob walked over and sat beside her.

"Well...?" he said.

Marie stood up and walked over to her dresser where she pulled a letter from her jewelry box. She hesitated, looking at the paper.

"Would you like something to drink?" she asked, not looking up.

"Whatever," he said, reaching for the folded paper.

Marie handed off the letter as she exited the room. Jacob could hear her let out a faint whine as she closed the door behind herself.

For the next few moments, Jacob read through the letter. Several times his hand dropped to his lap while the other rose to rub his forehead or wipe his eyes. Marie returned with a glass of water and handed it to Jacob.

The room remained silent as Jacob read on. He tossed the letter aside a couple of times as if he could read no further. After taking a sip of water, though, he would again pick up the paper. Marie stood with her back to him, sniffing.

When Jacob finished the letter, he lay back on the bed and wept. They both sobbed aloud; he on the bed and her face-down on the dresser.

Several moments had passed, then Jacob asked, "Why, Marie...Why?" The tears began to flow again. Without warning, the glass Jacob had been holding shattered, cutting deep into his palm.

With puffy eyes, Marie made her way to Jacob's side. "Are you O.K., Jake?"

He pulled away.

"I'm sorry...I'm sorry," she said as if guilty.

"I'm fine. It's not your fault." Jacob wiped at his hand a couple of times before the adrenalin faded back into grief.

"Why didn't you just tell me the truth?" he moaned.

"I was afraid of losing you," she replied.

"Don't you see, Marie?" he asked, "Now, not only do I have to deal with what's happened, but I also have to deal with your deceit!" Jacob' voice escalated to near frenzy, "I might have been able to accept your actions, but then you tried to cover it up, too!"

"Is it any worse than what you'd done in the past?" Marie countered.

"I told you about that! I came to you and told you about it," Jacob argued, "and I did it because I wanted to. Because I wanted to build something wonderful with you! I didn't want anything hidden that could destroy us!"

"Well, you waited four months before you told me. That sounds like you tried to hide it, if you ask me!"

She was right. He hadn't admitted it to himself then, but now he knew...she was right.

"If you would have asked me, Marie, I would have told you!" he proclaimed. "I wouldn't try telling half-truths or try skirting around it like you do – like you always do!"

"Why do you stay with me, then?" she begged, starting to cry. "If I'm such a terrible person, why do you stay with me?"

The question silenced him. After a moment of thought, he replied, "...Because...I love you."

Marie dug deeper, "*Why* do you love me? If I'm always hurting you...Why do you love me?"

Jacob couldn't answer. His mind was racing wildly, searching for the answer. Was it her beauty? Many women are beautiful. Was it because of the way she made him feel when he held her; the way they could kiss without ceasing...for hours without end, just kissing?

Was it the way she made his spirit lift with a simple smile? Were these reasons for love...or the *results* of love? He couldn't give an answer.

"I'm leaving," he said. She followed him to the bathroom where she dressed his wound. Then he walked out.

Even though their breakup happened years before, the memory was permanently etched into Jacob's soul, surfacing regularly.

It wasn't often that Jacob talked to himself aloud; that was for senile people. But now, as Jacob lay in the bed of his Brownstone Apartment; as he lay in the void of light, he did anyway. He needed to talk through this. He had to try to deal with it.

"'Why do I love you', Marie? Well...for years now I've been asking myself that question over and over. I think I can give you an answer now." Jacob paused briefly to find the right words.

"I understand *now* that love isn't about whys or why-nots. Love either exists or it does not. It's kind of like life...you're either living or you're not living. There are no 'whys'."

He paused again, trying to find better words.

"True love is also not the result of whys or why-nots. People don't love because of what others do to or for them. If someone likes receiving gifts, do they automatically fall in love with anyone who gives them a gift? No, not if we're talking about true love. It just doesn't work that way with 'the real thing'. On the other hand, if a person hurts another, love is not destroyed. As a matter of fact, the reason it hurts so much is *because* of love. Does that make any sense, Marie?"

Jacob's blanket was beginning to gather warmth. He shifted onto his side under the covers.

"You've heard it said, 'You can't make someone love you', right? Well, it works the other way, too. When you truly love someone... nothing can make you stop loving that person. It's kind of like God's love. It's unconditional. He certainly doesn't love us because of something we've done. He doesn't love us for what we do or don't do. His love for us simply exists. He even loves us when we're 'dirty'. He may not be happy with our actions and he surely wants us to live in a better way, but he still loves the imperfect us. When it comes to God, we often tend to think, 'gee, if I could only get control of this one thing, or if I would only not do those bad things, or if I could only bring myself to do that one good thing; then God will finally love me'. That sort of thinking just isn't based in reality. He loves us now...just as we are.

'Why do I love you', Marie? I can only answer by saying...because I do. I don't love you because of what you've done that's made me happy. And I don't *not* love you because of what you've done that's hurt me. Marie...I just love you."

The relationship was over. It was lost forever. Marie had moved on. Once a woman has her heart ripped from her chest, there is no resuscitation. There is no coming back.

For the moment, though, Jacob found some peace. Perhaps it was in the assurance of God's love for him. Perhaps it was his addressing the issue that he had tried to ignore for so long. Sleep would eventually follow.

Jacob spent the rest of the evening with Marie. No tears of sorrow or regret were shed; not in his dreams.

5

SQUIRRELS WERE chasing each other around; leaping from ground to tree and back again; crashing through the fallen, crisp leaves. It was a dance that Jacob watched time after time with endless fascination. The acorns were ripe for harvest and the playful little critters seemed to not so much compete *for*, but to *celebrate in* their reaping. It was entertainment at its finest.

So that's what people did before TV came along, Jacob thought.

A light, cool breeze caressed Jacob's skin and ran its fingers through his hair. He leaned back against the base of the tree under which he was sitting, closed his eyes, took in a deep, relaxing breath and enjoyed the moment of peacefulness. This was where he found joy: where a few simple things all came together in harmony. He wished he could stay in this state of euphoria forever, but the sun was rising overhead. Morning was burning fast. He set aside the assignment on which he had been working and pulled out a clean sheet.

Jacob put pen to paper.

Dearest Mother:

Your little Boilermaker thought he would drop you a line. Hope this letter reaches you well. Everything is going fine here.

My scriptwriting Professor just reviewed my first script. Some good feedback. She says I need to focus more on "showing us" instead of "telling us". Guess that means I need to use more descriptive, flowery language and describe what's going on instead of just telling what's going on. I should be a little less direct. She also said that some of the alumni from here have gone on to do some professional work. More than one person from here has written scripts for TV shows that we've seen. Wouldn't that be cool if your baby boy could do something like that some day?

The rest of my Professors are ok. Not learning so much about "stuff" but rather learning "how to think" more effectively.

Got more activists protesting the Iraq thing. They're saying "No Blood for Oil". I suppose it's ok, in their opinion, for a ruthless dictator to overtake another country...as long as it isn't America. Maybe that's why it's so easy for them to be critical – it's been awhile since we were at the mercy of someone else. We've become too proud...too secure. Anyways, I guess it's the "hip" college thing to do: protest something – protest *anything* and *everything*. There's even a group on campus called "The Damned". I infiltrated their pilot meeting just to see what they're all about and discovered that their sole purpose of existence is to tear down Christianity. They have no goals for themselves; just to belittle and try to uproot those who believe in Christ. They aren't going after Jews (with the exception of Jesus, of course) or Muslims or Hindus...they target only the followers of the cross. I don't understand why they would go after anyone like that. It seems insane to me. What do they gain from that?

In one respect, I guess we're mostly responsible for creating a group like "The Damned"; for having such a group after us. We've made and continue to make a lot of mistakes...guess that's why we need a Savior in the first place, huh? It's unfortunate that God takes the beating for our screw-ups. If only they would be clear in their attacks and come after us specifically instead of attributing our actions to God. If they really studied the matter they would see that Christians are the problem with Christianity, not Jesus or God's whole plan. God's love and intentions are pure and just...we're crap, aspiring to be more like Him, but often failing miserably.

You remember me telling you about Pastor Jack, right? Well, he's still going strong. Sometimes I wonder if he's actually escorting more folks to hell than he's diverting from hell. I know that if I hadn't had any true exposure to God before hearing that guy speak, there's no way I would ever want to know anything more about Christianity, based on what *he's* saying. "The Damned" should hire him as a recruiter.

There are so many different voices – so many different ideas – down here. But don't worry, Momma, you didn't raise no fool. I remember everything you and Dad taught me.

Anyways, enough of that. Dante and I joined a new club on campus that just started up. It's the Purdue Bass Fishing Club. I guess later this year we're going to have the first ever Big 10 fishing tournament against IU. We'll show them how it's done. It's just us two to start off with, but we're hoping that, if it goes well, we will eventually have a true Big 10 tourney; including Minnesota, Wisconsin, etc.

You've always been there for me. I can never thank you enough for that. I know it was tough and I wasn't always a little angel. You had to be both the enforcer and caregiver...not easy to do, I'm sure. But you did it well. I hope someday I can be your strength and take care of you.

I know you don't like to talk or even think about such things, but if you should happen to meet someone who is kindhearted yet strong, you certainly have my blessing to pursue him. It would be a little weird for me, of course, but you deserve a good helpmate...wish I could be there more for you.

You mentioned in your last letter that you saw Marie the other day. I understand she's engaged. I'm ok...yes, it hurts, but I'm ok. I hope he's a good man who treats her well. Wish I would have cherished her as she so much deserved, but I had to seek out greener pastures. Haven't found any. Biggest mistake of my life so far, but I'm sure I'll make more.

I think I've come to the place, though, where I can better accept things as they are. I've got a new motto, Momma: "It is what it is." My relationship with Marie was great, I didn't see how great it was, so now *it is what it is*. Everything "is what it is". If we don't like what "it" is, then we only have a couple of options: do what we can to make "it" what we want "it" to be, or, if that's not possible, let "it" go and accept "it" as it is. (Sorry about all the quotation marks.)

I know, Momma; I'm sure that's kind of confusing. I'm not sure I totally understand it myself just yet. Chalk it up to the philosophy course I'm taking. I don't buy everything my professors are peddling, but I can certainly learn from their methods.

The campus is beautiful. I love fall. The leaves have already turned here. Those yellow, orange and red colors are so beautiful. Temperatures are getting down into the 40's at night, only 65 right now...dry, crisp; perfect.

Hope to see you soon. I'll be home for Thanksgiving for sure, maybe sooner. Take care and call or write often.

Love ya,
Jacob

6

IT WAS a shame, Jacob thought, missing out on Professor Verloren's discussion today about existentialism. Last Tuesday's coverage of Zeno, though, should satisfy his philosophical needs for quite some time. One discussion about how "all is one" and "motion is just an illusion" was enough for Jacob.

Zeno...what a nutcase!

No, Jacob was taking a day off from Philosophy 101. It was one of those required courses that had slipped through the cracks, but taking it now did afford him a bit of variety and humor amidst his focused studies. Today, however, he would gain distraction from another source.

"The Boiler Room" was one of Jacob's regular haunts. Normally he would only come here at night with his pals, feasting on some of the world's best Buffalo wings and a few cold brews. But today, for some reason, he just needed to drink alone.

The just-off-campus pub was a welcome haven from time to time. It was decked out with Big Ten paraphernalia – Purdue, of course, taking center stage. Jacob liked the décor – natural pine walls and tables, varnished with a clear finish. Under the coating on each table were pictures of former athletes who wore the old-gold and black. Above the bar hung the coveted "I did the Big Ten" T-shirt for those ambitious enough to take the challenge of knocking back huge quantities of liquor. Purdue's signature drink was, appropriately, a Boilermaker. There was also the Bloody Hoosier (a Bloody Mary) for IU, the Furry Wolverine (a Fuzzy Navel) for Michigan, and other such cleverly named drinks for each of the eleven Big Ten schools. Any patron who successfully drank all of the listed drinks within the same day would be bestowed the honor of his or her own "Big Ten" shirt. Perhaps today, with such an early start, Jacob would become a proud owner. The thought crossed his mind to go for it – to get that shirt – but soon his mind began to wander. Where it led him took him far away from the sophomoric world.

What a joy it would be to be drinking a beer with my dad right now. With that thought, Jacob was wisped away to the dreaded past.

Jacob's father was a great man. He was hardworking, often on the job from before sunrise until nearly sunset, and often six days a week. Not being a "professional", Paul Dickens had to closely watch his finances. For a person of his salary, though, he provided well for his family. When he simply couldn't provide something, as was sometimes the case, he kept his family from *feeling* need. As a young child, Jacob thought that "gravy bread" was a weekly tradition – perhaps an old family recipe – but, actually, it was a necessity.

When his workday was over, Mr. Dickens made time to play catch with young Jacob; taught him how to throw the curve. In the summertime, Dad would make special arrangements to be at Jacob's baseball games. He might have to trade hours with someone or work 18-hour make-up days, but it was worth it to see his son play. If necessary, Mr. Dickens would go back to work after the games to finish up on a few things...but he made every game.

Coupons were as prevalent as cash in Mrs. Dickens's purse. They had to stretch every dime but, by doing so, they lived pretty well. Jacob never owned a handheld LED football game like some of the other neighborhood kids, and he certainly never had one of those expensive game consoles...but, just give him a cane pole, a shovel and an empty tin can to hold the worms and he was good to go all day. Because of his parents' hard work, Jacob's mother was able to meet him when he got home from school and spend all day with him during the summers.

Back then, Jacob had less...but less was more. In those days, happiness was real. Today, Father lay in a casket.

Jacob, now seventeen, choked back his tears as he listened to the eulogy at his father's funeral. Dad was only 39 years old; he'd never get to hold his grandchildren. The pastor spoke of Paul Dickens's love, dedication, and sacrifice. Paul took his family of three to church every Sunday and always taught them to show compassion for others. It was that compassion, Jacob thought, that lead to his father's death.

Paul worked...used to work for the utility company. He drove a truck around the county, restoring outages and performing routine installs and maintenance. Some might look down their nose at Mr. Dickens's choice of profession; a mere blue-collar worker. As far as Jacob was concerned, Dad was a hero who deserved to wear a cape.

Just let one of those hoity-toity folks try to dial 911 sometime when a line is down and we'll see if they still think his job was insignificant.

While Fort Wayne will probably never be listed among even the top 50 most dangerous cities in America, it did have its rundown areas. And, of course, those areas had service needs from time to time. It would have concerned Mrs. Dickens had her husband told her some of the close calls he experienced on the job, but he never did share those stories. No need to cause any worry.

Three days ago, Mr. Dickens had been working on a line from his bucket truck behind one of the city's "tuck-a-buck" saloons. It wasn't too unusual to hear a bit of ruckus in this part of town, even during the daylight hours, but today Paul's attention was drawn away from his work by the sound of a woman's cries. He noticed a young, long-blonde-haired woman with mascara bleeding down her cheeks screaming at some greasy punk in a muscle shirt. Paul could tell that her actions, while quite dramatic, were actually defensive in nature. The man was the aggressor...and this was not *just another argument*.

"Hey!" Paul barked from his lofty position. The couple, while being within range of hearing the shout, was isolated within their own present situation and carried on, oblivious to their surroundings. Mr. Dickens began lowering his bucket. Something was definitely not routine about this confrontation. During his descent, Paul saw from over the corner of the building's roof an elderly businessman walking towards the club. He shouted out to the gentleman to call for the police. Hearing the urgency in Paul's voice, the old patron scurried into the club to report the issue.

Outside, the scene quickly escalated and the young lady began taking quite a beating from the rough-looking man. Paul didn't know the woman at all but, based on her flashy attire, he assumed that she

31

was one of the establishment's dancers. Apparently, the anonymous scumbag had somehow lured the young lady outside, perhaps promising her some recreational pharms or maybe more cash. Whatever the bait used, it certainly wasn't his true motive. From what Paul could hear, the man figured that he had donated enough money to the stripper and now *she* needed to show a little appreciation in return. She, of course, saw things a bit differently. The man began throwing her around and soon had the girl by the hair, bent back over the hood of a rusted-out Chevy Nova; a butterfly knife to her throat. The already out-of-control situation was getting worse; so much so that Mr. Dickens leaped from his bucket several feet before it reached its cradle in order to intervene more quickly.

By the time the police arrived, the now-limping man had already fled in his hot rod, the bouncer was trying to piece the situation together...and the dancer knelt weeping over Jacob's dying father.

After the funeral, Jacob took his mother home. The car ride wasn't pleasant. Jacob wanted to be strong for his mother's sake, but he couldn't find any words of comfort. It wasn't like his father had died of old age; it was a tragedy. His father died defending a stripper! And they never even caught that "waste of flesh" who did it; a fugitive to this day, as far as Jacob knew.

"Well, Jacob," his mother said, "your Papa's in a better place now."

The tears began to flow like streams from both of them. Jacob could hardly see the road through his blurred vision. He never could understand why grieving people said things like that. Maybe it was just a way to begin the healing process.

"...but I want you always to remember," she continued, "that you have a mother who loves you...and, better yet, you have a Father who will never leave you." Jacob knew exactly what she meant.

It was a memory that Jacob relived often. It was like watching the same movie over and over again...only this movie wasn't a favorite, it wasn't pleasant and it wasn't replayed by choice.

The drinks were beginning to feel good...warm. The sorrows were still there, but now they were held down by the glow of an accumulating blood alcohol content. The sharpness of the pain was now just a tingle. Jacob would spend the rest of the day and well into the evening in his little corner of the bar, comfortably numb.

7

WHEN JACOB returned from class Thursday afternoon, he was greeted by a note clipped to his door: there was a package waiting for him to pick up. Not just a letter; a package! It was from Mom. It *had* to be from Mom! He stuffed his key and the slip into his pocket and rushed to the apartment building's office a few doors down. He must have looked like a real dork; like a school boy zipping along, wanting to run but commanded to walk.

Cool it, man; you're a college senior, not some stupid kid late for the bus.

Sure enough, it *was* from Mom. Jacob flashed his school ID to Judy at the office. She nodded and handed him a box. He scribbled down his name on the sign-off sheet, grabbed his bounty and headed back to his apartment.

Back inside, where no one could see him acting a fool, he tore at the packing tape with his bare hands. What could it be? He had never gotten a *package* from Mom before. Letters were great enough, but a package...that's just awesome!

On top, there was a letter; underneath, there were... Mom's homemade cookies! Jacob carried the box over to his coffee table and opened up the container of goodies. There was really no need for the plastic ware; no chance of the cookies going stale. That just wasn't going to happen. All the container was good for was to get the gems to him in one piece. The cardboard box could have done that on its own.

Jacob sank back into the sofa, holding half of a cookie. The other half was already rapturously bursting forth joy inside his mouth. Handel's Messiah was playing inside Jacob's soul.

He held the cookie proudly over his head as if he were some ancient warrior reveling in a hard-fought victory. "Hallelujah! Hallelujah!" he sang out, a few precious crumbs flying out of his mouth along with the muffled sound. Just then, another student was passing by Jacob's open living room window. She didn't stop or look in his direction, but if she had been a cartoon character you would no doubt have seen exclamation points and question marks popping above her head.

For a college student who's been surviving off boxed mac and cheese, fresh baked *anything* is good. Mom's homemade cookies, though, were "the bomb"!

Jacob thought, for a brief moment, that it would be the right thing to do to save half of the cookies for Dante.

He better frickin' hurry up about it if he wants any. Mom only sent two dozen...she...she only sent one *dozen cookies. That figures to six for you and the other...six for me.*

Jacob laughed to himself as he unfolded the letter.

My Dear Son:

I hope you enjoy the cookies I packed for you. Don't eat them all in one sitting and make sure you share them with Dante. Shame on you, I know what you're thinking!

Thanks for writing. I love you and always love hearing from you. It sounds like everything is going well. I am so proud of you and know that, whatever you do in life, you will succeed. You are already a winner in my book.

I think I understand what you say about "it is what it is". I guess I agree with that.

Here's a story about cookies that your pastor told one time and I thought I would share the message with you. I'm not sure if you were away at school at the time or what, but I don't think you've ever heard this one. So here it is.

My cookies taste great; I know you know that. You have always loved them. I remember when you used to help me make cookies. You always loved that, too. Remember how we would take the sugars and butter and beat those together, then add some eggs, salt, baking soda and flour? You helped measure everything out and put them together in the right order.

Here is what I want you to think about. Imagine you are making these cookies with me. Take the sugar first. White sugar and brown sugar. Taste just the sugars. They are both sweet. They are both different, but good. Yummy. Put them into the mixer. Now take the butter. Taste just the butter. Not too tasty, huh? But still ok to eat. Not going to have a meal of butter, but a little is ok. Put the butter into the mixer and beat it with the sugars. Now, taste the raw eggs. Kind of yucky. Put them into the mixer and mix with the other stuff. Now, taste a bit of salt (not too much, bad for your heart, HA HA). How does that taste? Sometimes good, but not too much or it will overpower. Taste the baking soda (I know you know what that tastes like, remember the time you put 1 cup in the cookies instead of 1 teaspoon?) Yuck! Last, taste the flour. Pretty plain, huh?.

Here is my message to you, my son. Life is like a cookie. It's made up of all kinds of different "flavors". There are great things, ok things, and yucky things. If you remove any one of those things, though, the end result is all wrong. But if you take everything as it is, it can be delicious in the end. I guess that is what you kind of mean by "It is what it is". Maybe? I don't know.

But I hope you enjoy the cookies. And think about what I've said. I know life can be tough at times, but you've got what it takes. I love you. Write me again. You know how I love your letters. Call me, too, sometime. I still like to hear your voice.

Hope to see you soon,
Mom

8

"LIFE IS GOOD" and "Life ain't always fair": both are true. Last night was more of an "ain't fair" kind of night. Dante, Whitney, Sue and Jacob were discussing the matter over far too many dime beers. It was Friday night, classes were done for the week and so it was off to the Boiler Room. It was free wing night at the pub, so it would have been almost sinful to miss it.

The weekend kickoff gathering had become a ritual. So much so that they always got the same four-top. It was *their* table. No one else dared take it. Jacob and Sue would sit together on one side, Dante and Whitney on the other. They would eat, drink and sing along with the blaring tunes playing through the massive speakers overhead. Jacob and Sue actually sounded quite good together. Their voices melded into a sweet harmony.

The two couples weren't really "couples" at all; not really. Even though the four were paired up, it was just a thing. These weren't the early blossoms of a lifelong love relationship for any of them. It was one of those "it is what it is" kinds of things. Still, it wasn't hard to tell that Whitney had always been "sweet" on Dante; more than he would have liked to believe.

"Where do you think you'll be five years from now, Dante?" Whitney asked him.

"I better be a damn executive of some corporation or something, smokin' cigars and livin' the real deal!" Dante exclaimed. "I've put in my time here, I've studied hard enough…time for some payoff, man!"

"Sounds a lot like entitlement," Jacob interjected, with a smirk.

"What the hell you mean by that?" Dante returned. "I'm serious, man. We worked hard; we expect to cash in from that, right? Otherwise, why we doin' what we're doin'? I say it's only fair that I get some bennies after all the time and effort I put up."

"For real!" Sue agreed.

"I'm just sayin' you need to be careful not to sound like some of the lemmings that go here," Jacob explained, "It's not the certificate that matters. Ya got to back it up with something. Contribute. Don't be a lemming, man."

"That's easy for you to say, man, you're white!" Dante countered. It was a recurring line and a running joke within the circle of friends, but each time it cracked them up. The saying was versatile and Dante used it at any given time for a good laugh. For example, if Jacob and Dante were sitting at a crossroad, trying to get into the flow of some heavy traffic, it would come into play: "C'mon, he's white!" Dante would say. Or they might be in line for tickets at the movies and someone would cut ahead of them in line. "Aw c'mon, can't ya see he's white!" Pulled over for a speeding ticket? "But he's white!" Dante always kept things rolling and the phrase was always good for a chuckle. Even now Jacob nearly choked trying to swallow his beer. He was tapping his plastic cup on the table as if slapping his knee.

Whitney jumped in, "Aw, screw it...let's just rob a bank."

"I'm in," Dante said, gulping down his latest cup. "We'll go in, guns blazin'. Sue and Jacob can keep the deuce running out front."

"Count me out," Sue exclaimed; leaning back, looking down at her drink and shaking her head. "I don't play like that!"

Jacob smiled, taking another chug. "You've been watching too many movies, Dude. If you're going to do it, do it right. The object of robbing a bank is to *not* get caught. You'd be cuffed before you reached the front of the teller line."

Sue and Whitney tried to suppress their giggles. Jacob was right and they all knew it.

"Not if I was white!" Dante returned. The girls couldn't hold back any longer and burst into laughter. Whitney grabbed for a napkin to tidy up some resulting dribbles.

"Alright, smart ass! Tell me how it is, Mister Republican. How do *you* do it?" Dante continued.

"I can't tell you, Bro. You're just crazy enough that you might actually try it."

"No way, man, give it up. If you're so smart, please share! We could be sippin' margaritas in Cabo by morning," Dante begged.

They all laughed.

"Hey, he *did* find a way to turn the tables on that thug at the liquor store, Dante," Sue interrupted. "I wouldn't put it past Jake to find a way of pulling off a robbery himself."

"No doubt, that's the sort of stuff you see in movies," Whitney added. "That was some fast thinking!"

Dante agreed, silently but clearly, with a raised eyebrow as he tipped his cup. That's what he liked so much about Jacob. Jacob was surprisingly "smooth" for a white farm boy; a "real playuh" when he wanted to be. The two young men hit it off shortly after becoming roommates. It seemed like they'd been best friends their whole lives. Jacob was Dante's "Brutha from a different Mutha", as he put it. The feeling was mutual, though not expressed in the same sort of words.

"Honestly, I got lucky. My mind was racing in all directions at that moment. I don't even remember consciously coming up with the plan...I just did it. I got dealt pocket rockets on that one," Jacob explained, taking another drink. "Now if ya wanna talk about what's not fair, check this: I catch a thief, then end up having to quit my job because he might have friends on the outside that would give me a special payback visit. Now that sucks! Where's the justice in that?"

"Man, I'm just glad you didn't get whacked," Dante pointed out. "We're too young to be doin' funerals."

Everyone at the table sensed that the conversation had drifted way too close to the boundaries of Jacob's painful past so they all made an unspoken, but conscious effort to redirect it. Not wanting to let the evening spiral into lamentations, Jacob pretended to not even make a connection. But, underneath his unaffected front, the connection had been made...and it festered. The rest of the night went on just like any other Friday night on campus...at least on the surface.

The several beers that Jacob consumed the night before with his "posse", as Dante called it, weren't feeling near as good now. Thoughts of his father were still fermenting within. He would get into just such a funk from time to time – part of the balance of things, he rationalized; some good days, some bad. Just as he often passed time thinking about the mysteries of beer recipes and such, Jacob also relied on the occasional drinking binge to bring a counterfeit sense of relief to the endless thoughts. It allowed him escape to a place of false comfort – true peace is found elsewhere. Today, however, he wasn't so comfortable.

Jacob sat under the trees most of Saturday morning writing, thinking and trying to regain a peace of mind. Today, the football team was scheduled to play the Illini. The Old Gold and Black flew proudly over Ross-Ade stadium and the campus was flooded with anxious fans. Cars and vans sporting their teams' colors were backed up, bumper-to-bumper throughout the streets. Fans from the visiting team adorned their vehicles with orange flags, orange streamers, orange ball...oons.

Orange balloons? Instantly, Jacob was carried back in his mind to his childhood. He remembered that day – the day when Mrs. Courier's fourth grade class launched their balloons.

Jacob never did hear of anyone discovering his orange balloon. Most of the children didn't; only a couple of the students received responses. One letter came from as far away as Maine; a new record.

It's not surprising that my balloon was never discovered. That's the nature of things. There is no magic. Only the select few ever experience that sort of thing – miracles.

Out of nowhere, Jacob's father resurfaced in his mind. Was the stripper's life really worth his father's sacrifice? It was the million-dollar question. It came up every time Jacob recounted the event...and he was never able to answer it with a "yes". He often wished that he could have met the young lady his father had given himself for. He needed to know if there was anything worthwhile about the woman. He needed something...*anything* to justify the tradeoff.

Since he was on the subject of the past, Jacob also devoted some of his thoughts to Marie. Why had he not seen her worth? Sue was a fine companion at school, but no one had ever even come close to touching Jacob's soul like Marie did. Marie had moved on now. Once she got over the pain of heartbreak, she was over it; there was no coming back for the possibility of a repeat.

For the rest of the day, Jacob couldn't seem to think of anything but his orange balloon and the harsh questions it begged. It continued nagging him. What a fool he had been to actually think his balloon – his dreams – would actually pan out. What a fool he had been to believe that!

Later that day, "the fool" gave in to his compulsive desires and purchased an old-gold and black helium balloon.

You can't give up. You just can't stop dreaming!

The values that Jacob's parents had instilled in him as a child must have still lived within him, somewhere deep and buried in his soul. Why they sparked now, he did not know for sure. Perhaps he had hit the bottom...there's nowhere but up. Hope, faith, love...you must believe! That's what led Jacob to this point.

Not sure how long it could take for someone to discover the balloon, Jacob put his mother's address on the letter that he attached. She had lived in the same house for as far back as Jacob could remember and he had no reason to believe that *that* would change anytime soon.

He probably looked like an idiot kneeling on the campus lawn, but, at this point, it didn't much matter to him *how* he looked. Jacob held his new balloon at arm's length. The effects of the alcohol from the night before were wearing off, but now it was his spirit that fell numb.

"Father, I'm a broken young man. Teach me what you will."

Soon, the balloon was out of sight.

9

JACOB KNEW his mother would most likely not approve of what he was about to do, but sometimes you just gotta do what you gotta do.

I've got to know, Momma, Jacob thought to himself. *I've just got to try to make some sense of this; get some closure or something...anything. Not only can I not fathom why my father was taken away so soon, but even less why he was taken away at the benefit of a whore.*

It was late. Jacob had declined the usual Friday night ritual to harvest something that had reached its ripeness. He drove his car towards Indy; no radio playing, no distractions; simply focused on what needed to be done.

This day had been destined long ago. Though he'd never consciously thought about it, Jacob had always known deep inside himself that this day would have to come. The past, the inner turmoil, had to be dealt with one way or the other. Jacob ran a hand through his hair as he drove, keeping his eyes locked on the road ahead.

By the end of today, my beliefs will have changed to some degree. At one end of the spectrum of possibilities, I might totally reject that there even is a God. At the other end, I might even find healing and new purpose. No matter the outcome, I'm going to get some answers...and I'm going to get them now!

Momma, ever since the tragedy I've felt like my father's life was wasted on trying to save a piece of trash. Because of her selfish, undisciplined gluttony, she chose to get into a situation that ended in my father's death. This has been eating at me inside like a cancer. It is a weight I can no longer carry. It is a disease I can no longer bear. By morning, I will be whole. It will be resolved at all costs...maybe even at the cost of my faith. I'm hoping I can walk away from this able to believe that my father didn't die in vain, but rather with purpose. Just fair warning, Momma, this could be just another "balloon" incident; another disappointment...another dose of the harsh reality that we are alone and on our own.

Jacob fought the demons in his head as the miles passed by. He tried to formulate a plan; a course of action on how the night should play out and how he might evaluate the results. The more he thought about things, however, the less the whole plan made any sense. This wouldn't be like a true or false exam where there is clear evidence of truth or error. Tonight would be more like grading an essay...he just hoped he would be able to make a clear judgment on its meaning.

Jacob had finally arrived at his destination. It was a "gentleman's" club on the outskirts of Indiana's capital city. He probably could have found such an establishment closer to campus, but he needed a pure sample. If he would have gone to a place near Lafayette, he most likely would have been studying his peers – college girls who figured they might as well get paid to flash their breasts. A less shrewd co-ed might normally do that for free any given weekend at any given bash. No, Jacob wanted...he *needed* the real deal. He was looking to study the true stripper; a stripper just like the one his father offered up his life for. He needed to know if there was any shred of worth...any *tiny* shred of value to the sacrifice.

It was Jacob's first time inside such a club. His buddies had often invited Jacob to join in for a night out at the booby-bars (not realizing the painful connection), but Jacob was always prepared to be conveniently booked in advance. "Aw man, sorry. I already have something going on," he would say.

The club, while not being in the best area of the city, actually had a slight – very slight – touch of class about it. It was dark inside, but each small table had a lit candle on it and was surrounded by comfortable, wheeled sofa chairs. Jacob grabbed a beer from the bartender and made his way to one of the two-seater tables in the back corner of the club.

The DJ was spinning a variety of music that Jacob hadn't heard in a few years – some old "glam" rock mixed in with more recent hip-hop tunes. "Put your hands together for *Mercedes*, gentlemen...She'll be heading over to stage two...Next up on the main stage we have the *lovely* Carley," he said as he cross-faded the beat to the next song.

As Jacob settled into the first few sips of his beer, he realized that he didn't really know where to start his investigation or exactly what to do or what to look for. This experience was entirely new to him and it was going to take some getting used to. The conflict inside of Jacob was still present, but it began to take a backseat to all the energy going on around him. He initially took in his surroundings –

the layout of the place and such – but soon his focus turned to the stage.

The DJ was correct: at least on the outside, Carley truly was lovely. Her appearance was striking. It gave Jacob a feeling that he didn't anticipate he would have; after all, he was here on business. Yet he couldn't help being drawn to her. She wore a red satin top, some silky white forearm coverings with frilly streamers and a mini-skirt to match. She stood on what had to be at least 8 inch heals. It was amazing that she could even stand on them, yet her moves were graceful, fluid, smooth...feminine. She seemed to become the music.

The pendulum swung. *What is your problem, man,* he thought to himself. *Remember why you're here. What is that...that girl doing up there? That's someone's daughter! You're sick, man! Get hold of yourself!*

Across the way, Jacob noticed one of the entertainers giving some dude a lap dance. Like the others, she was flashy. But it was a veneer; cheap gold plating on an aluminum core. It had to be. This girl was probably some spoiled teenager who never grew up; a brat who disrespected her parents; a rebel without a cause, thinking of no one but herself. She cared for no one. She sought out her own pleasures, in spite of anyone else's wants or needs, at any cost to others. She was a glorified panhandler; a dirty slob holding out her hand to grab anything she could. She needed to pump herself full of drugs. She would claim it was to kill the pain; she was a victim of society. Yes, Jacob could clearly see what she really was. His father was robbed of life.

"Need some company?" the sugarcoated voice asked.

Before Jacob realized where the voice had come from, a young dancer had already sat down at his table. She had a surprisingly peaceful look to her and a pretty smile. But Jacob would not be fooled; she was just another counterfeit of a human being.

"Uh, yeah sure," he replied, still a bit shocked from her sneaking up on him. "Have a seat...uh, yeah, you're already...why not, that's why I'm here, right?"

She giggled at his obviously novice demeanor. He certainly was not a veteran of such clubs. "So, how you doin' tonight? Havin' fun?"

No, he wasn't having fun. Actually, he felt kind of sick inside. How dare she even talk to him?

"Would you like a dance?"

"Uh, No," he replied. He imagined that he may have even had a distasteful, slightly upturned lip when saying so.

What made her think that that would even remotely be OK? Who was *she*? *She* killed his father! Well, maybe not her specifically, but it was someone just like her, essentially.

The girl sprouted a playful bottom lip and began to rise from her seat to move on.

Hold on, man. Remember why you're here! Fine, it seems pretty obvious that you were right about these flesh-sacks being worthless trash, but put some of your schooling to use. Put them under the microscope and prove to yourself once and for all, scientifically, that some people on the earth just aren't worth the dirt they're made of. Get the indisputable evidence, man!

Jacob shouted so loud that the young lady nearly spun a 180. The bark of his command came out as if he was listening to deafening music on headphones and didn't realize how loud he was speaking.

"Wait!"

The outburst even surprised himself, but he successfully downplayed it. He quickly pulled a fifty-dollar bill from his wallet and slapped it down on the table. He needed to get control of himself. *He* was in control of this situation, not her. He was the prosecuting attorney getting to the truth of the matter; proving the defendant guilty.

Play it cool. You've got to keep her around long enough for her to incriminate herself.

"I want to...I *need* to know you," he said.

She got a disturbed look on her face now. "Sorry, bud, you gotta go downtown for that sort of thing...you think I'm a whore or something?"

"No, no, I mean, I want to know *about* you."

Still a bit suspicious, the young lady moved over to Jacob. She leaned over him and pushed his chair back up against the wall. She took a step back and began to sway to the music, then reached behind her neck with both hands and began to unfasten her top.

"No, no, wait! Keep your clothes on. I want to get to know you...I just want to talk to you. Just sit and talk with me," Jacob explained.

She paused, shrugged her shoulders and then plopped down into his lap. "You look like a decent guy and all, but...whatever... Sure, let's talk. Um...what would you like to talk about?"

Face-to-face with her, Jacob found himself a bit disarmed. He didn't really understand that. He thought that he would be enraged in such a position, but he wasn't. He kicked the fog from his head and focused.

"I want to know your story. Tell me your story." Jacob could see that his request made her feel uncomfortable; displaying the unrest of someone who really, *really* didn't want to reminisce about her past.

"Look, I'm a college student," he said. "I eat macaroni out of a box most nights. I have to buy the cheap beer. It's taken me a long time to save up the cash so I could come here." He could see that she was still not digging this. At one moment it appeared that she was ready to just get up and leave.

"Let's start here: I'm Jake. What's your name?" Luckily for Jacob, he *did* come across as a nice guy; the young lady softened a bit.

"Samantha...well, actually it's Rose, but I go by Samantha here. Nice to meet you, Jake." She gave him a little squeeze around the neck instead of a handshake; a little different.

She better knock that off. She doesn't know what's really going on here. Calm down...play the part, man.

"You're a friendly one, that's for sure," he joked. "Nice to meet you too, Rose. So, where ya from? Did you grow up here in Indy?"

"Actually, I was raised in Brazil." Her answer was noticeably short. Jacob suspected a bit of apprehension on this topic. Stranger still, Rose certainly didn't appear to be of South American decent.

"Hmm. Well, not to be ignorant or anything...and it's not that I don't believe you, but you don't strike me as a Brazilian."

She's lying! Strike one! Now it's starting to come out.

"I was raised in Brazil," she stated again as a matter of fact. This time, he could hear the sincerity in her voice. OK, so maybe she wasn't lying. It was clear now, for certain, that this was a touchy subject, so he redirected.

Gotta keep her around longer...not enough dirt on her yet.

"OK. So, let's see...have you been doing this sort of thing long?"

Rose began to display a bit of tension and her words sharpened.

"What...do you mean have I had a *job* very long? Yeah, I used to be a waitress. I've had a job for several years now, doing one thing or another; gotta feed my children, right! It's a job, and it keeps the bills paid."

Yeah, well being a hit man is a decent paying job too, he thought, *but knocking-off folks like my father just ain't right.* He felt his blood pressure rising and his cheeks and ears most likely turned a shade of red at the thought of it. *Strike Two...or is it still One? Doesn't matter; I hope she burns...*

He stopped himself. A wave of conscience slammed into his soul. Where did *that* come from? Did he really want her – want *anyone* – to burn in hell? He couldn't even finish the phrase in his head. Had he become like Pastor Jack? Had he *been* Pastor Jack all along when it came to his father's death?

The preconceptions that Jacob had formed on the drive over were beginning to fade...slowly, but they were fading. He had come expecting to meet hard-looking, worn out, *strung* out tramps; not people who seemed relatively human. Sure, their attire and the setting was a bit wild, but this *person* almost seemed real. Some of the girls were obviously on something, with their glazed-over eyes and all. But a handful of them, like the girl in his company, seemed *maybe* a little different. *Maybe.*

Rose sensed something in Jacob's silence and expression, but she couldn't figure out exactly what he was thinking. He's probably another "judger", she thought. Either that or one of those guys who was here to save her; a "savior" who offers no *real* solutions. She grabbed Jacob's cash and stuffed it into his shirt pocket and, without a word, got up to leave.

"Whoa, hold up there, friend."

Did I just call her 'friend'?

Yes, he had...and compassion was starting to stir within him.

Where is your heart, man? What if she is...real? What if?

"Rose, don't take me wrong. I'm not here to condemn you. Well, at least not *now* I'm not. Let me tell you a little about myself: This is my first time to a club like this, as you can probably tell. I don't really want or need to get into the details, but I really needed to meet you. You've already helped me understand a few things and I want to know more."

Rose could hear the sincerity of Jacob's voice, but she was hesitant to feel at ease. She lowered herself back into his lap, but didn't make herself too comfortable about it.

"You sound like you don't really like what you're doing," he said.

Jacob seemed like a genuinely nice guy. *Do those really exist?*, Rose thought. Going against her conditioned defenses, she opened up a bit more. Her arm was again reaching around the back of his neck and resting on his shoulder.

"Well, no, not really...there are a lot of assholes in here. And sometimes doing what I do really makes me feel worthless. But, like I said, I have to take care of my children."

"Have you ever thought of getting a degree or doing something else?"

"Jake, how am I supposed to raise two children, earn a living, and go to school all at the same time? I'm only one person." Rose was calm in speaking this. It was how things were. It was a matter of fact.

Jacob reached for her open hand and took it into his with compassion.

"Don't you have any family around to help out?"

"No, no family." Rose sighed, looking to the ceiling. Again, it was obviously a sore spot.

"What about a shelter or a church or something... government assistance? Don't you know anyone who can help you out? I mean, if you really don't like what you're doing...you don't see any way out?"

Rose looked away from Jacob and cleared her throat. She began to emotionally drift.

"I'm done with church and organized religion. I don't like talking about this much, but my father was a missionary in South America. He's gone now; all the better."

Jacob was pretty shocked to hear that Rose was raised in a religious environment. It was clear that she didn't hold any endearing feelings towards her father. She didn't clarify, but based on her body language and attitude, Jacob considered that the group she was raised by could have been one of those poisoned-juice-drinkin' gangs. It wasn't worth the risk of asking her, though.

Rose directed the hand holding hers back to Jacob's lap; essentially telling him that he was incapable of understanding.

"As soon as I was old enough to leave, I did. Then, when we got back to the States, my husband left me with the two boys. This job is the most money I can make without having a high school diploma. 'Would you like fries with that' just ain't gonna get the job done. There are too many bills and I want my children to have *something*."

Rose paused, cautioning herself to not blame this decent stranger for her pain. She straightened a few of Jacob's stray hairs with her free hand.

"Don't get me wrong, I do believe in God, but the church ain't for me. I've seen too much crap. So...I just pray with my kids each night before bed. Maybe He'll hear us someday."

Jacob didn't know if all of what Rose had told him was true (although she sure seemed to be sincere) or even if she may have contributed to her situation somewhere along the line; it didn't really matter at this point. What he *did* believe, though, was that this poor person was in a tough situation and didn't have a whole lot of hope to change matters.

"You've really made me think about some things, Rose. I wish there was something I could do to help, but I'm at a loss."

Wow, she thought, now *that's* different. Jacob was probably the first guy she ever ran into in this place who didn't seem to have it all figured out for her. He didn't have a 12-step program to change her life. He didn't try to become her Sugar Daddy Savior; with strings attached, of course. He didn't even want her to take off her clothes.

"You've already helped," she said with a smile. "You've been a real gentlemen...not many of those in here."

Jacob rubbed her back. He was overwhelmed with compassion. He couldn't believe that she had touched his heart and he certainly didn't understand it.

"Take care of yourself, Rose. I wish you well." Jacob said, handing her back the money.

"I don't want your money, Jake."

"I want you to have it. I know it was difficult for you to tell me all of that."

Rose paused, looking squarely into Jacob's eyes. She took his face gently into her soft, warm, moist hands and just stared into his eyes for a moment.

"I really appreciate you treating me like a real person," she said.

She leaned over, kissed Jacob on the cheek and politely excused herself.

10

D ANTE WAS ALREADY at the apartment when Jacob arrived. He had some ramen noodles simmering on the stove, but it was only a single serving according to Dante's stomach. Jacob was going to have to fend for himself.

"Whaddup, Brutha?"

"Hey, Dante. You have a good day?" Jacob replied as he closed the door.

"Just another day in paradise. You got a letter from your momma...didn't send us any cookies this time," he laughed, pretending to wipe crumbs from his mouth.

"Ha, ha! You're crazy, man."

Jacob dropped his backpack next to the couch and fished the letter from the pile of mail on the kitchen table. The envelope was larger and a little heavier than normal. Jacob gave it a squeeze and shook it.

"No, probably no cookies this time," Dante said, amused by Jacob's childlike behavior.

"Yeah, that's what you'd like me to believe," Jacob accused, jokingly.

Jacob carried the letter to the living room, plopped down into the recliner and slit open the envelope. Inside was Mom's weekly handwritten letter along with a second envelope. The additional letter was from a person in Bloomington whose name he didn't recognize.

"Hmm...looks like one of the Hoosiers is in need of some masterful assistance again. They're so helpless," he said, flashing the address to Dante. Dante laughed.

"Who's Angela?"

"Probably just another one of my fans," Jacob joked as he ripped his finger down the fold of the envelope.

Jacob pulled out the letter and began to read it. At first he looked confused but, as he read further into it, his face lit up.

"What is it, man?" Dante asked.

Jacob looked up at Dante, his eyes wide and mouth agape.

"Dude! Someone found my balloon!"

"What? Balloon? You been smokin' something without sharing. What you talking 'bout a balloon?"

"No, uh...man, you might think this is wacked or something, but you ever heard of people trying to find pen pals using helium balloons? It's like a message in a bottle kinda thing."

"Uh...naw, man."

"Yeah, people do that. I sent a balloon last fall like that with my mother's address in it. Long story. I guess someone found it. This is totally awesome, man!"

"Must be a white thing," Dante snickered, still a little out of the loop.

Jacob was consumed with the letter, so much so that he wasn't really listening to Dante; otherwise he would have at least cracked a smile. He took the letter to his bedroom to read it more thoroughly.

There wasn't anything real earth-shattering about the letter; pretty standard stuff coming from a stranger. It basically said that this young lady, Angela, had found his balloon and decided to write back. She told a little about herself and asked for the same sort of basic information from this Jacob person she was writing to. She included a return mailing address and an email address as well. Jacob decided he would go to the library later to email her back. First, though, he would tell Mother.

He went to his desk, pulled-out a sheet of paper and grabbed a pen from the drawer.

Dearest Mother:

Can you believe someone found my balloon? Yeah, you know that letter you forwarded me? It was from someone who discovered my balloon! I'm going to run to the library shortly to email her. I had already given up hope on the balloon idea, since it's been almost 3 months since I sent it off. Guess I need to learn to be more patient. I'll keep you up-to-date if I hear back from her.

Hope all is well with you. I suppose this is normal for someone my age, but I've really been struggling with life lately. Don't worry, I'm ok...guess I'm just going through a learning and growing season. This balloon thing helps...gives me some hope. But I guess it kind of bothers me that it took an event like that to make me feel that way. It seems a bit like a crutch...I should have hope, patience, peace, etc. without

59

depending on some sort of "sign" like that. I know you've always said that God has everything under control and nothing happens without going through Him first. My professors would certainly disagree. They attribute things to chance. No offense, Mom, but I'm not sure where I stand on that. I do believe that God is out there watching over us...but some things that happen to people just don't make sense. Much of the time the wicked prosper while good folks struggle. That doesn't seem right to me. You might say that God destined for someone to find my balloon; that He ordained it because He felt I needed a shot of hope to get me through. Others would say the wind blew the balloon and by <u>chance</u> it landed in a populated area and by <u>chance</u> someone found it and by <u>chance</u> that person responded. Maybe they're right. I'm really confused right now. Sure, someone found my balloon, but if God has a plan for everything like you say, then why didn't anyone find the balloon from my childhood? See what I'm saying? Sometimes stuff just happens and other times when we want things to happen they don't.

Here's what I'm talking about. Aunt Judy is a good person, right? She goes to church every week, she prays all the time, as far as I know, she's never hurt anyone. I get a birthday card from her every year without fail. I get Christmas cards, Easter cards and quite often she just sends me a letter for no evident reason whatsoever. She is a good, kind person...who has cancer. She doesn't smoke...never has as far as I know. She's kept herself healthy and seems to eat right. She has cancer. She cries out to God for help or answers...He

60

seems to turn a deaf ear. She "sends out a balloon" several times a day, every day, but it always seems to end up in a forest or a lake, or who knows where. You might say that if it's God's will to heal her, it will happen when the time is right. She needs help *now*! She needs answers *now*!

We are His children, right? I need to be careful with this, and don't take this the wrong way, I'm not slamming God, but I honestly don't understand this. If I had a child who *really* needed help, I don't think I could just sit around and do nothing...just sit there and watch it happen...watch my child die; whether that be physically, emotionally, or whatever.

I can hear you saying it now, Mom, that "we will never fully understand the mystery of Him and His ways"; that "there is a time, season, and reason for all things". I'm trying to believe that.

I've been thinking about Dad again. This goes back to that growing thing, I think. I feel like I'm at a turning point on that, but it hasn't totally settled in yet; kinda like wet cement...it's there, but it's not yet reached its final form. I think I'm able to deal with his passing better than before, but it's still tough. I'm sure it always will be. At one point I was like, "my dad got killed because of some idiot whore". But now I'm feeling more like, "my dad died, even for a stripper". Some day I hope to get to the point of "my dad sacrificed himself for another person who rightfully needed help." I'm not there yet, but I feel I'm evolving there.

Sorry about all the heavy talk. I really am fine. The fishing tournament is happening this weekend. It's on like

Donkey-Kong! Ha ha! Sorry about that Momma, you probably don't get that, and no, I haven't started taking drugs. It's just an expression. Never mind. Dante and I are in the same boat. That rocks! I'll give you a call you after the weigh-in and give you the details on just how badly we filleted the Hoosiers.

I'm gonna go email Angela now.

Love always,
Jacob

P.S. Send more cookies!!!!

11

"WHAT ARE YOU throwin', man?"

"I'm gonna start off with a crank bait", Dante replied as he tied on the artificial crawfish.

Jacob always preferred fishing with soft plastics; a Texas-rigged night crawler being his favorite. But since it was springtime, he followed Dante's lead and switched-over to his other rod with a crank bait. Jacob never really understood why they were called "plastic" baits. As a child, he knew them as rubber worms. It made sense; they were rubbery, not plastic. *Plastic is hard, isn't it?*

The Indiana Chapter of Bass Masters supplied the boats and drivers for the first-ever "Old Minnow Bucket". The name of the fishing tournament was a play on words coming from the "Old Oaken Bucket", the ceremonial trophy of the annual rival football game between IU and Purdue. It was a clever and fitting name.

The Bass Masters were instructed to simply transport the two-man teams to the location of their choice, but not to offer help or any advice. "Team Flounder", as the two Boilermakers chose to call themselves, decided to troll the shoreline on the nearby south bank for starters. As soon as the starting gun was fired, their driver, Bob, put the motor to the test and zipped his team quickly to the opposite shore. Within what seemed to be mere seconds, they were in place, trolling motor engaged, and began pounding the shallows.

"Alright, man, let me take you to school," Dante said proudly as he made his first cast.

"Whatever, dude!" Jacob laughed. "You couldn't catch a cold in the Antarctic!"

The weather, overcast with a light rain, would have been perfect for fishing had it not been the case for the past several days. When a low-pressure front first comes into an area, it seems to drive the fish wild; turns them into piranhas. But since this was about day four of the same climate, it seemed like the catch had gone to sleep. Nonetheless, Team Flounder was having the time of their lives. Their environment was a cold, wet swamp; their spirits were a tropical paradise.

"So who's this chick you been talkin' to?" Dante asked.

"Well, this *young lady* is named Angela," Jacob corrected. "She's about to graduate from IU with a nursing degree. She seems to have more than her share of character, too."

"And you met her via balloon?! What's up with that? Your email broke?"

Bob the driver didn't have any of the back-story, but when overhearing Dante even *he* laughed aloud.

"Well, yeah," Jacob said with an abundant smile, "I guess we did originally, yes."

"That's some crazy shit, man! I gotta shoot straight; you got a new sparkle in your eye lately. You goin' soft on me?"

64

"Relax, man, I haven't even met her in person yet. We exchange emails about every day and she is really an interesting person. We have a lot of common interests."

"What she look like? She sent you a picture?" Dante asked.

Jacob couldn't contain the burst inside – the smile broke free and he began to blush.

"Aaaaah...Uh-huh!" Dante accused, "she's hot, ain't she? She *HOT*! I got your number...interesting...uh-huh...lot's of character...yeah!" Dante slapped his knee as he laughed.

The whole boat broke into laughter. Dante could be such a clown. He was professional and "all-about-business" in class and formal settings, but just get him into a casual setting and watch out! He was like a leech that, once it got hold of something, would not let go without some serious intervention.

"C'mon, man," Jacob said. "I *do* like her personality and we *do* have similar likes. The looks are just a bonus."

"Mmm-hmmm!"

"OK, Dante, how 'bout this? I'm meeting her soon for dinner. We're *just* having dinner. I really enjoy talking to her, but if...*if* it ever goes beyond that, you'll be the first to know. Well, ok, *we'll* be the first to know, but you'll be next, alright?"

"Appreciate it, man." Dante said, adding, of course, one of those looks you might give a child who swears his hand was *never* in the cookie jar. "Whoa!" Dante pulled back hard and fast on his line, it felt like dead weight.

"Got something?" Bob asked.

"Uh...not sure, might be...no I'm hung up," he replied, somewhat disappointed. Dante tried to pop the lure loose, but the line snapped.

"You deserved that, man, pickin' on me like that," Jacob teased. "Karma's coming ta get ya!"

Bob and Jacob exchanged satisfying winks...Dante got his just deserts.

"Oh, ya think so, huh? It was fate, huh? You believe in that stuff, don't ya?"

Dante reeled in his line and quickly switched to his backup rod, back in action in a flash. "You think your balloon thing was fate too, I'll bet."

"No, not really. How 'bout let's talk about *you* for awhile? Have you told anyone yet about how you cheated them out of some lures and other 'fabulous' prizes?"

Dante stopped reeling, looked Jacob in the eye and they both busted out laughing.

A couple months back, the Bass Fishing club had a fundraiser that Jacob was involved in. It was his idea to have folks donate a dollar to guess the number of plastic worms in a jar. The winner would receive a box full of donated lures and other fishing supplies. Being in charge of the contest, Jacob counted the number of worms and wrote the total on a piece of paper from his notebook, making sure he pressed extra hard when he wrote down the number so it would leave an indent on the pages underneath. Then he tore out the sheet and stowed it away until everyone placed their entries. The members looked briefly at the worms and made their best estimate, writing down their guess on a scrap piece of paper. Dante, *of course*, didn't have any paper with him, so he borrowed Jacob's notebook for a piece. Jacob remembered giving Dante one of those "don't be stupid enough to guess the exact amount" looks. Amazingly, when the final entries were tallied, Dante had come within 14 worms of the actual total and walked away with the treasure.

"That wasn't right," Jacob said, laughing. "God's gonna make us pay for that one some day."

Just then, Jacob felt a jolt. It felt as if he had just been struck by lightening. He was momentarily paralyzed. "Fish on!" he yelled. "...I think. No, I think I'm hung up, too. Oh my God!" What felt initially like an anchor on the other end of his line was now pulling back, forcefully. Jacob's reel started to sing as the line peeled off. Bob cut the trolling motor and Dante dropped his rod. Almost immediately they were by his side, coaching him as he fought the monster.

"Don't muscle him!"

"Treat him like the black man...don't give him any slack!"

"He's jumping, steer him down!"

"That should be *my* fish!"

"Take your time, be patient!"

"Holy crap, look at him! Let him run a little!"

"Keep wearing him down!"

"Oh sure, let Whitey catch the big one!"

Five minutes and 1000 exclamations later, the nearly six-pound black bass was in the live well. Jacob did a victory dance and, even though he would have loved to own the bragging rights for himself, Dante joined in.

The weather was dreary, the wind was biting, the action was slow, the catch was few; what a perfect day! The Boilermakers won the first ever "Old Minnow Bucket" that day and Jacob was crowned with Big Bass of the tournament.

12

THE DAY had finally arrived; the day Jacob and Angela would meet in person for the very first time.

In one of her first emails to Jacob, Angela explained that her grandfather had passed away in late March and she was helping her parents clean up the farmhouse. One day she had been in the barn, cleaning out much of the stuff that her grandfather had pack-ratted over the years. She had climbed up the ladder to the hayloft and was shoveling down massive amounts of old straw and hay that had become unbundled over time. While doing this she had noticed something wrapped around one of the rafters high up in the loft. It was Jacob's balloon.

For the past month or so now, the two had been corresponding by email. They had reached the point of learning some of the more personal things about each other. Angela was twenty-two years old; Jacob twenty-three. Both she and Jacob enjoyed watching old black-and-white movies. They both liked quiet winter nights, bundled up in front of the warming glow of a fireplace. They liked the simpler things in life.

Not since Marie had Jacob met someone with so much depth and transparency. Most of the people Jacob encountered throughout life seemed shallow. They seemed like parrots, regurgitating only what they had heard on the latest fad sitcom the night before. Their small talk bored him and their safely structured, politically correct conversations were a waste of his time. Angela, though, spoke from within. She shared what was on her mind and in her heart, with little regard to how others might receive it. She was the real deal.

Now that the school year was over, they could finally meet in person. Angela and Jacob decided to have dinner at a nice Italian restaurant on the North side of Indianapolis. Jacob drove down to Indy from Fort Wayne. Angela had a shorter trip from the Bloomington area. They both arrived safely at the designated time and place.

When Jacob first saw Angela, he was captivated by her beauty. She was even more stunning than in her pictures. Her curly, auburn hair was held back by a golden clip and looked like a lava waterfall, cascading down to her shoulders. The lights from the restaurant's candles sparkled in her deep aquamarine eyes. Her ruby cheeks were surrounded by the fairest, ivory flesh. And her lips...her burgundy lips looked like the velvety petals of a rose.

Jacob met Angela in a welcoming hug. She fit well into his embrace. Jacob wanted to keep his arm around her, or at least take her by the hand, and walk her into the restaurant. It was a first meeting, however, so he anxiously escorted her inside without doing so.

The atmosphere of the restaurant was perfect. The lighting was pleasantly dim, accented by candlelight throughout. Patrons

70

enjoyed each other over a low hum of conversation with an occasional silverware crescendo. The tablecloths were of the purest white and the aroma of freshly baked Italian bread was nearly intoxicating.

Angela had the Melanzane Parmigiano and Jacob ordered Capellini con Funghi Fresca. Neither of them were vegetarians, though it may have seemed that way by what they ordered. They sampled each other's selections and agreed that they had made outstanding choices. Both dishes were far more impressive than the canned raviolis they had been surviving on for the past four years in college.

After dinner, Angela and Jacob sat for hours, talking and enjoying one another's company. They began to feel at ease with one another. Jacob told his story about how he had nearly lost his faith; how he was really struggling with this whole God thing lately. He explained how, in one last effort, he decided to send off a balloon; to "leave it to the wind". It was amazing enough that anyone found his balloon in the first place, knowing how remote the chances actually are. But for his balloon to be found by someone who seemed to so closely fit his dream of the perfect woman, for someone to find his balloon "just in time"; for someone to feel the same way about him as he felt about her...it was truly incredible. It was a wonderfully romantic story.

"You see, Jacob," Angela said, "your mother is right. Trust in God and He will work things out as they should be."

"Yeah, I suppose so," he replied softly, lowering his eyes to the table.

"Jacob?" Angela asked, concerned; reaching across the table and taking his hand.

"I'm sorry...I *do* believe in God," he said weakly, "but don't you think it also could have just been chance? Maybe we are all alone. I mean, it's not totally impossible that all the variables were just right that day to carry the balloon to you. Bloomington isn't all that far from West Lafayette. The wind generally blows in that direction."

Angela paused for a moment, studying his forlorn expression with probing eyes. "Can I ask you a question, Jacob?" she finally murmured. "How would you feel about God if I had never found your balloon? What if your balloon had floated a couple of miles away and fallen into the Wabash River, never to be found? Would you still believe in God? I would hope that you don't need to rely on 'signs and wonders' in order to have faith."

Jacob didn't answer. He squeezed Angela's hand and forced a smile.

"You know," she continued, "God doesn't always do things the way we would...or the way we might like. I don't know why God took your father away. I don't know why your Aunt is suffering. I don't even know if His hand was in me finding your balloon. I guess that's something you can ask Him in the future."

Jacob still didn't look convinced.

"You know the story of Job, right? I'm sure you've heard a few sermons in your life about him. You know...the old message about perseverance."

"Sure, of course," he replied.

"Well, maybe you should read that story again. When I read Job, I get something completely different out of it than what we usually hear from the pulpit. Normally we get the standard message of 'hang in there and God will restore you', but there's another message that seems to get passed over."

Jacob tilted his head to the side with a look of curiosity.

"Well, you know that Job had everything taken from him – *everything*. His friends showed up to comfort him and kept saying things like, 'You must have sinned really bad to have such things happen to you'. Job replied over and over again that he had done nothing wrong, that he loved God and that God must have made a mistake...that God was not treating him justly. Here's the part that seems to get passed over. After Job kept repeating such things, God came to him with a strong message. God said to him, and I'm paraphrasing here, 'Job, if you're so smart...if you think you know me so well, instruct me how to create the universe, show me how to contain the waves of the ocean, move the stars in the heavens, create a beast for Me and feed, shelter, and protect it.' Basically, God was teaching Job that He is far bigger – far more capable and in control than we can ever imagine. He was basically telling Job that we're not always going to understand, from the human standpoint, why God lets things happen the way they do, but not to worry. He is more than able to let things happen as they should...and can do things far more amazing than we think."

Jacob's eyes began to light up. It was a tough message, but it brought him some comfort in strange, powerful way.

"Wow," he exhaled. "That's deep, but I think you're right. I've read the Book of Job a few times but never got *that* message from it. I'm really starting to believe our meeting was destined, and not just chance. God truly *is* amazing."

A radiant grin spread over Angela's face. "Yes, this could have been all because of chance or luck or whatever else you choose to call it. But I personally believe God was in on this one, too. It's just something I sense. And what's even stranger is that I feel He's not done with this lesson yet. He can do so much more than help us find a balloon. I can't put my finger on it, but I feel like He's saying to us, 'How much more have I done than you *think* I've done?'"

Jacob rose from the table to meet Angela in a hug.

"You are wonderful," he said, giving her a kiss on the cheek. He moved his chair around the table to sit close to her.

"Jacob, you cried out to God to teach you something before you released the balloon, right? Well, what have you learned?" she asked.

"I've learned that there's a wonderful young lady named Angela. She's beautiful and fun to talk to and to be with. And I'm glad I sent that balloon," he added.

"Me too," she giggled. Her rosy cheeks reddened.

"You have to admit, it's pretty amazing where that balloon ended up," Angela said. "I mean, the opening to my grandfather's hayloft is probably only about fifteen feet tall by fifteen feet wide. If it would have landed somewhere outside of the barn, there's no way I would have *ever* found it. There are woods, creeks, and fence rows all over the place. That balloon had to land just perfectly; must have got sucked right into the opening. And there must have been an upward draft too inside the barn to get it up to the point where it finally rested. That was one heck of a shot, Jacob!"

"Yeah," Jacob laughed, "from where I let it fly, that was a pretty decent shot...well beyond the 3-point line."

They both laughed.

"You know what's really amazing about this story, though, Angela?" he asked, continuing the humor. "It's that a Hoosier responded to a letter attached to a Boilermaker balloon."

"I'm not sure what you mean," Angela said curiously.

"The balloon..." Jacob explained, "I sent the letter attached to a gold and black balloon."

Angela looked puzzled. "The balloon, Jacob, was...orange."

Psalm 46

__Matthew's Prayer__

"Father, turn this Vinegar I've made into Wine."

"Sometimes God puts gold under my shovel, so I dig."

Matthew W. Bertsch (1968) was born and raised in Fort Wayne, Indiana. He presently lives in the Dallas-Fort Worth area of Texas.

From an early age, Matthew loved to create. He spent much of his free time capturing stories on his mother's cassette recorder. In high school he focused his creativity on producing video shorts, winning First Place at the Indiana State Media Fair and Honorable Mention at a National Competition in Atlanta, Georgia.

In 1992, Matthew earned a Bachelor's Degree in Telecommunications (specializing in scriptwriting) from Purdue University in West Lafayette, Indiana. His poem "Heritage" was published in the 1992 Purdue Exponent Literary Issue.

Matthew's first book, <u>Jacob's Balloon</u>, centers on lessons he learned throughout his life. He has a blog link on his website where readers can submit their own thoughts regarding some of the discussion points and mysteries of the story.

You can check out his website at:

bigdaddywrites.googlepages.com

Special thanks to my blessed and loving family; to the one who is "Marie", the one who loved a fool; to my incredibly talented editors Laura Dungey and Tammy Hardy; to Richard for constantly reminding me to dream; to the Norbergs for teaching me invaluable lessons, lessons they don't even realize they've taught me; to Anne Joline, you inspire; to Robin, a friend; to Dusty, you have a spirit of sweetness; to Rose, be blessed; and to Pastor Chandler and those at the Village for "keeping it real", for giving me *real* food and a *real* home...

...but most of all, big-ups to "The Winemaker"...You know who You are.

www.ingramcontent.com/pod-product-compliance
Lightning Source LLC
Chambersburg PA
CBHW020637130626
46552CB00003B/1279